Footprints

in the

Mind

ISBN 0-935906-04-5 (Hard cover)
ISBN 0-935906-00-2 (Soft cover)

Footprints In The Mind

Javan

This book is written

For those individuals
    who gave me my Dreams
And especially for those
    who gave me my Memories

Walk gently through the pages of this book, for here you will find many well worn paths, and some may even bear your footprints. If you should find a particularly familiar path, do not hesitate to pause long enough to say ''I've been there before''

She loves me

I speak
  Because I know my needs
I speak with hesitation
  Because I know not yours
My Words
  Come from my life's experiences
Your understanding
  Comes from yours

Because of this
  What I say
    And what you hear
May not be the same

So if you will listen carefully
  But not with your ears
To what I say
  But not with my tongue

Maybe somehow
  We can communicate

Should I offer but a smile
Please don't be disappointed
So many give -
a lot less

Someday I will smile
    And find the warmth of my smile
        Reflected back to me
Someday I will reach out to someone
    And find that I only have to reach halfway
        For she will be reaching out to me
Someday I will find
    The true meaning of the word Love
        That many use so carelessly
Someday I will find
    Someone with whom I can share
But for now I must try to know myself
    And the world around me
So when the time comes for me to give
    I will know the meaning
        of my gift

She loves me not

Time is the essence of all life
This is especially true
In the relationships between people
As more time is spent with someone
The feelings toward that someone
Become more defined
As with parents, teachers, and friends

So please don't think of me
As a Stranger, but as someone
With whom you've never shared any time
If given this opportunity
You might learn to feel toward me
As you do toward your friends
And loved ones

I didn't know her, but she smiled
And from her smile - a warmth
    Seeped deep inside me
I knew no words, that I could say
      Yet, I think she understood
And in the coldness of that lonely day
She had given more
    Than most ever could

Because I took a moment to speak
And you took a second to smile
A tiny part of me will leave with you
And a little bit of you will stay

An attraction between two people
               can happen spontaneously
But a lasting relationship
              takes work

She loves me

God grant should I never find
The comfort of a woman's love
In my short stay
That I learn to appreciate
Enough of life's beauty
That this one shortcoming
Will not leave me wanting

I am an idea
Conceived in the mind of the Universe
And interpreted in the minds
of the individuals I meet

Within myself I am constant
Yet I am as ever changing
as the people who interpret me

I can control my actions
But I can not control their thoughts
Therefore, I must do what I think right
And let others -
Think what they will

Life comes in the form of opportunities
Which are easy to recognize
  - once they have been wasted

It starts
At a time called birth
And continues
Till a time called death
It is called Life
It comes with no guarantees
''Of 60 years or 60 thousand miles
whichever comes first.''
And somehow
They've even left the instructions out
Yes, all we get
Is Life itself
And it's up to us
To do the Living

In a world so full of wonder
With so many exciting things to do
It's a shame
So many choose to just exist
Rather than to live

I find it hard to understand
Others as they come and go
The words they speak, the things they do
Are things I just don't know

But I think I'll try to fool them
And do things differently
By trying just to understand myself
And let them - understand me

She loves me not

In my lifetime
    I hope to develop

Arms that are strong
    Hands that are gentle
Ears that will listen
    Eyes that are kind
A tongue that will speak softly
    A mind full of wisdom
A heart that understands

It's not so much a matter
 of meeting the right person
As it is meeting them
 at the right time

How frequently it is
That out of humanity's crowd
Someone steps forward
To cross our paths
And just one look
Starts a funny feeling
Growing deep inside

And we wish
That somehow we could utter
A secret phrase
That would hold the world
Suspended in time
Until we could share a moment
And let our feelings be known

But the world turns so quickly
Taking each his own way
And the funny feeling of hope
Becomes a subtle sadness
Which we try to cover
        With a smile

Have you ever wondered
Which hurts the most
Saying something
　And wishing you had not
Or saying nothing
　And wishing you had

Lord - Please, quick
Give me a line,
    or something to say
That might start to explain
The storm raging inside me
    since she walked into the room
Just one line that will let her know
The feelings deep in my heart

Lord - Please try hard
And do better this time
For the last one wasn't impressed
With ``Hi Babe, what's cooking?''

From time to time
   A stranger appears
      And presses a button
         That starts emotions
            Churning within us
But it's not so much that person
As it is our interpretation
   Of what they can mean to our life
That makes our throat dry
   Our speech hesitant
      But worst of all
Makes us so very, very
                  vulnerable

Maybe someday I'll be lucky enough
To hold you in my arms
Rather than just in my mind
Maybe someday I'll trade in empty dreams
For the thrill of one night's memories

And the cold of the world
Will be shattered by your warmth

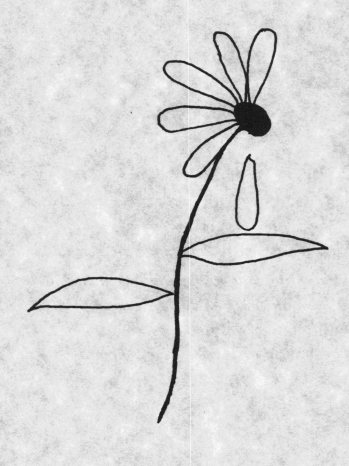

She loves me

I would not ask from you
    Anything that you were not capable of giving
I would not ask from you
    Anything but that which I truly need
And I would not take from you
    Without giving equal value in return

You are from your world
And I am from mine
    Two different worlds
In my need, I can hold you
But only in my mind
While other arms hold you for real
And I can only hope
His arms give you the enjoyment
That the dreams of you
    Give me

Should I hesitate in my steps
And I walk when you bid me run
Please understand
I've stumbled before

When you plunge into the water
And you urge me to jump right in
Please understand
I've strangled before

And in the heat of passion
You bid me come to you
Please understand
I've been . . .
       please, just understand

Listen carefully to the words of others
For often very deep truths are revealed
clothed in jest

There are so many words
Yet there are no words
For when I look into your eyes
No words need to be spoken
And the warmth of your smile
Is a statement in itself
And how could I ever try to explain
The trembling in my body
When I touch your face

There are no words to explain an emotion
So I open to you my mind
That you might walk
Among my Dreams and Memories
Then . . .and only then
You might understand my silence

She loves me not

Can I live without you
Now that I know you
Now that I know you exist

Can I sleep at night
Without seeing your smile
Now that I've seen it for real

Can I be the same
Now that I've changed
With the gentle touch of your hand

Now that I'm divided
By my need for you
Without you
    Can I be whole again

How often the world introduces
People we never get to know
They walk right in, we see their smile
Then watch as they turn and go

We stand and scan the footprints
Their leaving left behind
And the departure of a stranger
Can leave footprints in the mind

Footprints
Four footprints in the sand
Waves washing to shore
The moon hiding behind flourescent clouds
A star for wishing
Indentions in the sand of two people huddled close
Silence - and yet conversation
The chill of the wind blowing in from the sea
Lights on distant ships
Hands -
    Holding -
        Touching -
            Caressing
The sun awakening across the horizon

Footprints
Four footprints running in the sand
As if tomorrow could never come
Laughter
A feeling of Happiness - deep inside
Living Life
    Giving
        Sharing

Tomorrow
Footprints
Two footprints in the sand
    Searching
        Remembering

I am an individual
    Completely unique
A composite of everything
    And everyone
        That ever touched my life
And tho I will not change for you
I cannot be with you
    Without being changed by you

Will you love me better tomorrow
Than you have through the night
Or will the early bird of morning
Take you with its flight
Will the sounds of our laughter
With no echo, fade away
Will tomorrow be - just a memory
Of the love we shared today

I'm just a man, much like any other
Playing a game
    Which is strictly ad-lib
        Not even sure of the rules
Going somewhere
    Without knowing where
Meeting people
    Who are gone too soon

And in the shadow of their departure
I become acutely aware of needs
That I have been afraid to acknowledge

Should I hesitate as I speak
Please don't think me preoccupied
For words don't come easily
When one really cares
And too often I evaluate each word
Trying to be anyone
            - but myself
And the fear of rejection
        Brings confusion
The confusion brings silence
And my heart prays
        That you might hear my silence
                - and understand

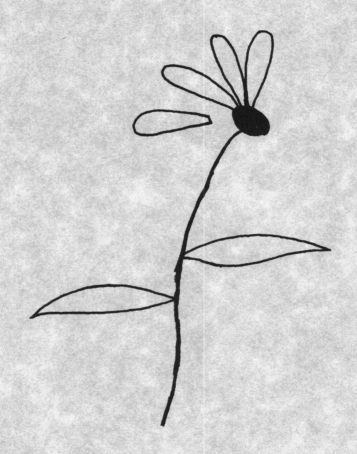

She loves me

Whether it was chance
  Or that thing called fate
    That brought you to me
I really can't say
  And I don't believe
    It really matters

For I have been lucky enough
To have the opportunity to hold you
Not just in my arms
But also in my heart

And should the winds of time
  Blow hard enough
    To take you from my arms
You can rest assured
  They will never
    Take you from my heart

Some people find it difficult
to say ``I love you''
While others find it easy
. . . sometimes too easy

Please don't ask me
    to say ``I love you''
For if you can't
    see it in my eyes
    or feel it with my touch
You will never
    hear it on my lips

Many days have come and gone
Since the day you shared with me
It was Our Day
A Red Letter Day for me

We shared much more than just time
    Laughter -
        Conversation -
            Silence -
You gave me reason to smile again
And be excited about tomorrow

Now, when sadness surrounds me
That you were gone so soon
I try to rejoice
That you ever came at all

Have you ever smiled
And said goodnight
When you were really
Saying goodbye

I woke early this morning
To the silent sounds of raindrops
    caressing the window
I pulled the curtain to greet the morning
But a fog covered the window
Without thinking I took my finger
And wrote your name in the moisture

Now, it was time to prepare
    to face another day
For some reason, just before leaving
I returned to the bedroom
To look once more at your name
But it too
      was gone

If I were to take stock
Of all my worldly treasures
The memories I have
Of the few hours spent with you
Would be my most cherished possessions

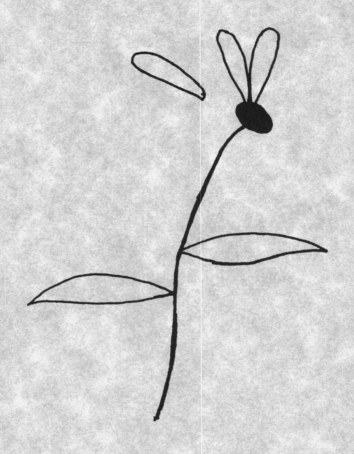

She loves me not

I've seen it before
    And I'll see it again
A couple just hanging on
    Even though the words
        Are no longer gentle
And the caresses
        No longer sincere

But the memories
    Of what once was beautiful
And the fear and uncertainty
    Of loneliness
Make them cling to each other
Long after goodbye
            Would be appropriate

Today
Someone asked me
If I had forgotten you
With a moment's thought and a subtle smile
I answered no

No, I haven't forgotten
The years we shared
When you gave to me
And I gave to you
And like everything else in life
Some was good
Some was bad

But to completely forget
Would create a void in my life

So even as I say
I'm over you
I have the strength to choose
Not to forget you

The time of my life
In relation to the world
Is insignificant

The time spent with you
In relation to my life
Was brief -
    but not insignificant

Oh-oh.

She loves me

You look in the mirror
At lines that were not there yesterday
And find a couple more hairs turned grey
With a nervous glance at me
You wonder if I notice ``Little Things''

Later, as I lay beside you
And sleep has closed your eyes
I think of the way you stroked my hair
And how, before you hung my jacket
You held it close to you

I reach out and take your hand
And with all the love the world has known
I bring it to my lips
For yes, I notice ``Little Things''

You came into my life
Unannounced
Uninvited
But not unwanted
You came at a time that I needed
A tender smile
A gentle touch
A woman's company
You came with understanding
For you asked no questions

With loving care
You healed my wounds
And nursed me to health again
Then you watched over me
Till I regained my courage
To face the world again
And in your wisdom you realized
My need to be free
So you tied no bonds

Now each night
Wherever I am
I think of you
Wherever you are
And in my heart I repeat
``Thank you''

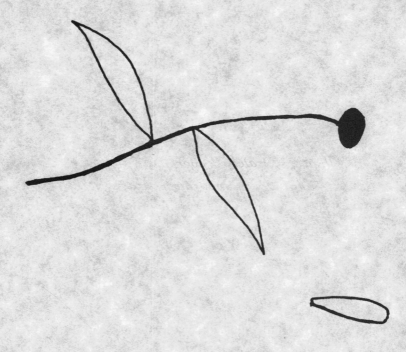

Oh, well. What does a dumb old flower know, anyway?

There are now four titles from Javan available
in a matched set: **Footprints In The Mind,
Meet Me Halfway, Something To Someone,**
and **A Heart Full Of Love.** Many bookstores
are now stocking these books; however, nearly
all general interest bookstores have them available
from their distributor and can get them in a few days.

If you should be one of the many people interested
in getting a book of poetry or even a single poem
published, but do not know how to go about it.
You should check with your local library and bookstores. So many people are interested in having
something published that many books have been
written to serve as a guide. These books will take
you step by step through the complete process,
and will explain to you what to expect. There are
also books that list all the places that are interested
in buying poetry.

*This page is written especially
for those of you
who read the last page first.
If, by chance, this applies to you
then you have found a special book
that will be cherished many years.*

Javan (which is the author's given middle name) was born October 19, 1946 in a small North Carolina town. He lived in N.C. through high school and college, then moved to Atlanta in 1968, where he worked as an agent for Eastern Airlines until the end of 1977. In 1979 Javan self-published his first book and started traveling around the country with a Golden Retriever puppy, Brandon, introducing the book to bookstores. There are four titles now available and Javan still travels frequently both nationally and internationally.

Unfortunately, Brandon died in 1988.

HAPPY BIRTHDAY!

Look past what you
see and look for the unseen.
Look solely for the truth. Take care
always. God Bless You!

Love in
Christ,
Maria